Journeys and flowers

ALSO BY MERCÈ RODOREDA

In Diamond Square
Camellia Street
Garden by the Sea
A Broken Mirror
War, So Much War
Death in Spring
The Selected Stories of Mercè Rodoreda

Journeys and Flowers

STORIES

Mercè Rodoreda

Translated from the Catalan by
GALA SICART OLAVIDE and NICK CAISTOR

With an introduction by HELEN OYEYEMI

Daunt Books

First published in the United Kingdom in 2024 by
Daunt Books
83 Marylebone High Street
London W1U 4QW

1

This work was translated with the help of a grant
provided by the Institut Ramon Llull.

LLLL institut
ramon llull

A CIP catalogue record for this title is available from the British Library.

ISBN 978-1-914198-96-0

Typeset by Marsha Swan
Printed and bound by TJ Books Ltd, Padstow, Cornwall

www.dauntbookspublishing.co.uk

Contents

TRUE FLOWERS

CONTENTS

INTRODUCTION

So you're about to go on a walk with Mercè Rodoreda. Or, if you're like me and only take a look at the introduction after reading the text proper, then the walk has just taken place. Well, what luck: we couldn't have picked a better day to link arms with one of the most charismatic flâneuses there ever were, her perspective fleet-footed even when (particularly when) her travel on foot was most urgent – fleeing Nazi forces as they approached her Roissy-en-Brie castle refuge in 1939, for instance. Consider Rodoreda's non-fictional account of what it was like to be part of a group driven at a frantic pace across landscapes that kept erupting and then erupting all over again: 'We passed over a bridge to Beaugency, which was being mined by French gunners. It was an afternoon with a very dark and very low sky. The Germans began to bombard the bridge with scary stukas; and you could see the bombs falling and exploding nearby.'[1] The group Rodoreda was in transit with was headed for Orléans, but Orléans was already on fire when they reached it, and all Rodoreda and her lover Armand Obiols could do was watch rubble burning from the window of a country house, fix that sensory shock into their memories and carry it into continued exile (in Limoges for Rodoreda and Bordeaux for Obiols). That wasn't even the first significant migration undertaken by this writer, whose multi-tonal range incorporates what Natasha Wimmer has astutely noted as 'a sadness that reaches beyond historic circumstances, a sadness born of helplessness, an almost voluptuous vulnerability'.[2] Just a couple of months preceding the flight from Roissy-en-Brie to Limoges, Rodoreda had left her home in Civil War-stricken Barcelona, where a number of those she loved had been killed or otherwise destroyed on the grounds of ideology. There was no reason to believe she wouldn't be next: 'I had never been in politics, but the fact of having written in Catalan, and for having collaborated in magazines, let's say on the left, etcetera, etcetera. And advised by my mother, because I left thinking that after three, four or five months I would return home, but then it became eternal.'[3] At least thirty-three years on – that is, sometime between 1972 and 1980, Rodoreda wrote *Journeys and Flowers*. It incorporates her view from quite a different country house to the one with the windows that framed a burning city. It's possible that in some way the book celebrates the author's risk-free return to Catalonia: it was written in her final home, the one she had built next door to her friend Carmen Manrubia's house in leafy Romanyà de la Selva.

The tales collected in this volume reflect the author's readiness to reinvent through fiction the long, long walk she had taken. It was clearly the sort of walk Henry David Thoreau championed in his essay 'Walking':

> We should go forth on the shortest walk, perchance, in the spirit of undying adventure, never to return, prepared to send back our embalmed hearts only as relics to our desolate kingdoms. If you are ready to leave father and mother, and brother and sister, and wife and child and friends, and never see them again – if you have paid your debts, and made your will, and settled all your affairs, and are a free man, then you are ready for a walk.

Thoreau refuted any relationship between civilisation and a walk of the magnitude he described, but Rodoreda expands the scope of ambulatory adventure so that it passes through all categories of nature, including the human. Having read *Journeys and Flowers,* I'm still on the road with Rodoreda, and with an indefinite return date, to boot. I've closed the book, yet the walk continues. As I write, cocoons populated by abandoned women and their attentive sons, a heroic purple flower who leads a rebellion against the wind, and the ticklish chagrin of a man 'who called down the lightning and when the lightning came it said it didn't want to kill him because he wasn't worthy of dying by fire' jostle the mighty curvature of a rainbow's humility: 'And the rainbow trembled, collapsing on the earth with one foot on either side and its back touching the sky.' My mind is aswarm with all these sights. You may find yourself in a similar condition. It wasn't possible to prepare for the revelry and unease of tumbling through Rodoreda's atlas of invented territories, and this is probably as it should be. My knowledge of wonder is far from encyclopaedic, but it does seem to be a good rule of thumb that if an experience can be anticipated or rationalised, you won't find the sublime there. Taking the opposite direction, then, the soliflore gardens of Mercè Rodoreda are rooted in the stuff. Somewhere around my third re-reading, I reached the opinion that *Journeys and Flowers* is a twice-translated text. The first act of translation is conducted with such skill and audacious grace that its seams are near-invisible; the scenarios that unfold here have the feel of verbal analogues for scenarios that were first depicted by leaves, buds and petals. And now these life-laden portraits have burst across the border of the English language, thanks to the simultaneously rich and airy, green-gunpowder dynamism of Gala Sicart Olavide and Nick Caistor's translation. We're reading the work of a writer who was fluent in her very own dialect of the language of flowers. I'm referring to an aspect of Rodoreda's literary persona that I discovered only recently, while seeking a sense of the quality and quantity of literary acclaim the author received in her lifetime. Those captivated by the psychological nuance Rodoreda's writing makes palpable in her novels *In Diamond Square* (1962) and *A Broken Mirror* (1974) were just as likely to hail the author's botanical ability. Twentieth and twenty-first century literary super-luminary Gabriel García Márquez, 'having been compelled to meet her by an irresistible admiration' of 'the sensuality with which she reveals things within the atmosphere of her novels' confessed to feeling so shy in her presence that it became necessary to pin his conversational hopes on the garden view from the window of Rodoreda's Barcelona apartment: 'I knew that, together with her literary vocation, she had a parallel vocation, one just as dominant as the other – that of growing flowers. We spoke about the subject, which I consider another form of writing.'[4] Márquez doesn't tell us what year this meeting took place, but it must have been after 1968, since he mentions an exchange of compliments revolving around details from Rodoreda's *In Diamond Square* and Márquez's own *No One Writes to the Colonel* (1968). This means that the prestige Rodoreda's romantic verse had won at the Floral Games of the Catalan language would have been a well-established aspect of her reputation. The Catalan Floral Games, modelled upon a springtime tournament of eloquence for troubadours first held in fourteenth-century Toulouse, awards flowers crafted from precious metals for outstanding verse on two types of love – love of country and love of divinity. The Catalan Floral Games awards a natural rose for verse in a third category: affairs of the heart. The natural rose is the prize that Rodoreda pursued and won three years in a row, before ultimately claiming recognition as *Mestre en Gai Saber* (Master of the Gay Science), the award given to the poet winning all three categories, in 1949.

Who else speaks the language of flowers, and what conversations does it allow for? It's not news to any of us that this is a language to which all kinds of lovers turn. Flower speech accommodates the raw ardour of fifteenth- and sixteenth-century Ottoman courtship and the more abstract communication formed in the mould of nineteenth- to early twentieth-century English sentimentality alike. Attempted adherence to the Victorian language of flowers was still going strong in the 1980s, as Brent Elliott of the Royal Horticultural Society's Lindley Library recalls:

> I compiled a little card catalogue of plants, based on the dozen or so period works we had in the library, so that if someone rang up to ask what was the meaning of, say, a crocus, I could quickly say: 'Well, it depends on what book you consult: it could mean Youthfulness, Youthful Gladness, The Pleasures of Hope, Rashness, Impatience, or Abuse Not'. To which, all too often, came the further query, 'But what is its *real* meaning?', and somehow, my standard reply, 'Plants don't have real meanings; its human beings who assign meanings to them,' was never perceived as adequate.[5]

The language of flowers is a language for lovers, and for the lost, assembling semiotic shelter out in the wilderness. No wonder that in Shakespeare's *Hamlet*, Ophelia speaks this language as she's increasingly unmoored from anything remotely resembling inner tranquillity: 'There's rosemary, that's for remembrance. / Pray, love, remember. And there is pansies, / that's for thoughts.'

The nameless narrator of 'Journeys' also knows what it is to stray onto paths of liminality. A fellow whose senses are, by his own account, all but fatigued by the iconography of revolution, he remains intent on discovering what liberty looks like to everybody else, and will not permit us to conceive of him as the source of these visions. Passing through the Village of Witchcraft and the Village of Hanged Men respectively, he politely reiterates his status as a reactive agent conveying impressions: 'My task is not to stop but to carry on forever; to continue the endless hunt for dark hearts and unknown traditions.' Epistemological limit-setting unites the two halves of this collection: the section entitled 'True Flowers' discusses the nature and character of various extraordinary blooms hellbent on surviving mundanity, but precludes exchanges with the flowers themselves. Our interlocutor's brevity and discipline steers us away from the fatal flaw of over-identifying with the poignant, recalcitrant, debauched or prim fragment of matter that merely appears to be the sole subject of the narrative. A candidate for co-subject: the tempestuous zone of commonality inhabited by all that can be gathered and scattered and everything that grows and withers, whether sentient or non-sentient. The very darknesses contained within these heliotropic imaginings swivel to face the light of the sun; in the dead of night the world still glitters with solar treasure that's been left in the safe-keeping of other entities: 'I found myself not beside the melodious spring, but on the shore of a lead-coloured lake which reflected in it the mysterious sliver of moon, glancing at me out of the corner of its eye and with a half-smile.'

As ever, all scintillation is transitory. In the first few pages of this book readers in the right state of mind will be charmed by the notion of a man serving as entertainment for the moon, whereas the latter pages are haunted by the intensely provisional existence of the Shadow Flower:

> When she is not even a shadow, lost in her flower, she remembers the drops of water from the sky as if they were a mirage. When the sun brings her to life, she thinks back to this. And when the moon brings her to life, she looks and looks at the black embroidery of water without even daring to breathe.

The nocturnal clarity of Rodoreda's 'Journeys' touches fingertips with the *outrenoir* paintings of Pierre Soulages, which can also be considered portraits of the spirit of our age. Soulages, whose most striking mission state-ment is possibly 'My instrument is not black but the light reflected from the black', also described a tangible effect of both his work and the vignettes assembled in *Journeys and Flowers*: 'I always liked paintings to be walls rather than windows. When we see a painting on a wall, it's a window, so I often put my paintings in the middle of the space to make a wall. A window looks outside, but a painting should do the opposite – it should look inside of us.'[6] Rodoreda and Soulages are artists whose traversal of time is even more significant than a trip around the globe. They are members of a generation who lived on terms of hair-raising familiarity with what David Rousset has termed the 'concentrationary universe', a period indelibly marked by consciousness or sub-conscious co-existence with the forms of inhumanity that flourished in the camps. The resonant speaking voices of Rodoreda's inventions in *Journeys and Flowers* (inventions that, just like the rats in 'The Village of Well-Bred Rats', study us every bit as keenly as we observe them) could lie in their sounding, like calls from the time before total war to the times that come after. The post-war universe is one that nobody alive right now can enjoy the certainty of visiting, though we can never say never – the hope and the desire for this is far from lacking. There's a chance that it isn't only lovers and the lost who speak the language of flowers, as well as the language of bright nights – it's possible that time speaks these languages too, and that the visions we encounter on these walks with Rodoreda are our chance to confide in the times we are living through, carefully tracing our own dreams and nightmares in between the lines that pass before our eyes. Don't forget the afterbloom of the final flower in this book: it lasts until all the trees have been transformed into crosses – it lasts until all that's left of the sky is a piece of blue.

Helen Oyeyemi, 2024

NOTES

1. Translation of an excerpt from a televised interview Rodoreda gave in 1980: *Mercè Rodoreda: A Fondo – In Their Own Words.*

2. Natasha Wimmer 'A Domestic Existentialist: On Mercè Rodoreda' *Atlantic* (2009).

3. *Mercè Rodoreda: A Fondo.*

4. Gabriel García Márquez and David Draper Clark, 'Do You Know Who Mercè Rodoreda Was?' *World Literature Today* 81, no. 3 (2007): 13–15.

5. Occasional Papers from the RHD Lindley Library 10: 3–94 (2013).

6. Pierre Soulages, *Interview Magazine* (2014).

JOURNEYS TO SOME VILLAGES

Journey to the Village of Warriors

I had to quickly step aside as around a thousand horses were coming towards me, a thousand soldiers carrying lances mounted on them. They galloped past, shouting and howling, raising clouds of dust. Then the beating of drums began. In the vanguard, chest thrust forward, head held high, came the standard-bearer. Red and white, his banner fluttered in the wind: inscribed in red letters on the white, and white letters on the red: VALOUR, PURITY.

Rat-a-tat-tat, rat-a-tat-tat . . . silver drums, golden shields, bare-chested soldiers. The sun was shining on their faces, and the glinting silver and gold made me close my eyes. The trumpeters kept up their calls. All of them rode by in perfect, disciplined formation. The swirling dust died down and settled on the ground. The world emptied, and there was a great silence.

I lay down on a bank covered in wild fennel and fell asleep. The sun, which when I lay down was burning my back, was burning my face when this great commotion woke me. I had to shrink back as around a thousand horses were coming towards me. A thousand soldiers carrying lances

mounted on them. They galloped past, shouting and howling, raising clouds of dust. Then the beating of drums
began. In the vanguard, chest thrust forward, head held
high, came the standard bearer. Red and white, his banner
fluttered in the wind: inscribed in red letters on the white,
and white letters on the red: VALOUR, PURITY.

Rat-a-tat-tat, rat-a-tat-tat . . . silver drums, golden shields,
bare-chested soldiers. The sun was shining on their backs,
so the glinting silver and gold didn't make me shut my
eyes. The trumpeters kept up their calls. All of them went
by in perfect, disciplined formation. The swirling dust
died down and settled on the ground. The world emptied,
and there was a great silence.

I asked an old man as gnarled as a vinestock, who was
ploughing a field just behind the bank of fennel, why all
these soldiers were marching up and down. It's always
the same, they come and go twice a day: morning and
evening. They live in tents some way from here, in an
olive grove. They don't bother anyone: they play at being
soldiers to gain respect, and everyone fears them although
all they do is gallop about and play trumpets. Their
women wait for them up beyond the olive groves; they are
all young and pretty, and shimmer like the reeds in the
riverbed. They all wear pearl earrings and a pearl set in a
gold ring, and the gold ring is on the big toe of their left
foot. All of them in their houses of porphyry and marble,

with blue roses climbing the trellises round their doors, waiting night and day for their menfolk, languishing from so much waiting while the men parade up and down ... rat-a-tat-tat, rat-a-tat-tat ...

Journey to the Village of Lost Girls

It wasn't a village, it was a wood. The girls had left their homes, some to go and pick clematis, some to pick poppies, some purple thistles, others dog roses, and had not known how to get out of the wood they had to cross, and the wood kept them. They were all dressed the same: a red skirt, and a jerkin with small blue and yellow flowers on a navy-blue fabric. They were all blonde, with corkscrew curls. They all had blue eyes, each of them had in their hand a bunch of the flower they had gone to pick. As soon as they woke up they began to dance round and round the trunk of a tree, each on their own, as they sang the dawn song. 'What do you live on?' 'On chestnuts, the ones that still have a smooth green husk, and every so often we snack on the ones with prickles.' One of the girls carrying a bouquet of jasmine explained her life to me: 'I had a good life at home, I had as many dolls as I wanted, I always ate young pigeons' brains and dishes of custard. When I was thirsty I always drank sweet almond cordial, I slept until I was done with sleep, and had more than enough time to dream I was a fish, a bird, a snake or a hyena . . . but one night I dreamed that the jasmine flowers were calling me; they wanted me and only me to pick them. They opened little by little, and from the tiny hole they have in the centre came a voice that was mine and said while I was asleep: *We want the girl who has everything to come and pick us before the bee makes honey from us.* I got up, it was the dead of night, sleep still in my eyes, all of me was enraptured, and I set off walking and walking until I found the jasmine, made a bouquet with all its stars and now I'm a lost girl because I never knew how to find the way back home, my home with its garden full of wallflowers and forest lilies.' I told her I could accompany her, I could accompany all of them one by one. Her face immediately became sad and the blue of her eyes, cloudy; she ended up admitting she preferred to be a lost girl and live in the wood where at night the branches of the chestnut trees drooped down to where she lay, wrapping themselves around and embracing her, saying they would love her until the hour of her death; that if she didn't leave the wood she would always be a girl with a red skirt and corkscrew curls like wood shavings, with the blue of her eyes full of watery tenderness, and drops of dew between the rose of her lips ... And she added, her eyes filled with innocence, and without blinking, 'Whenever a girl is lost, they name the village after her, and that girl becomes the patron saint of that village. They buy a big doll, dress it as a saint, give it a tin heart, put it in a glass case and visit it and bring it flowers from time to time. My name is Gertrudis.'

Journey to the Village of Abandoned Women

I sat on a milestone at the edge of the path to eat a snack, watching the flight of a female blue jay, in the venomous blue. I was chewing slowly, and when I lowered my gaze because I could no longer see the jay, my attention was drawn to a green wood, a spellbinding green, which spread from behind the edge of a field of barley, on the far side of the path. It was a strange wood, too forlorn, with no breeze, and the leaves on the trees so thick that from a distance the tops seemed covered in moss. I was surprised, as anyone would have been, that every so often a stone shot out furiously from the rounded treetops, falling heavily to the ground. Lots of stones flew out of the tangle of leaves as if this was some kind of game. I went closer, and when I was near I could see that all the stones were tied to a string. When I drew even closer I could see that as they fell the stones often got caught on a branch, and then someone pulled on the string and lots of leaves fell. I did not have to be very wise to realise that this game of stone-and-string was aimed at collecting leaves. Next to each tree was – little could surprise me after all I had seen in so many villages – a boy or a girl, aged around three years old, who was throwing the stones very skilfully. At the foot of the trees in a large silkworm-like cocoon, was a person. As the cocoon wasn't properly closed, the head of the person inside peeped out of the top. And that person was a woman. When some of the boys and girls became aware of my presence they stopped gathering leaves and stepped inside the trunks of the trees, which were open and hollow. They all looked at me, and the woman in the nearest cocoon, in a voice as slender as the thinnest silk thread, asked me what I was looking for. 'I, ma'am,' I said very politely, 'came to see what was happening with those stones that from afar I saw flying out of the tops of the trees.' One of the boys enveloped in a tree trunk laughed. The woman craned her very short neck and asked: 'Are you coming to keep me company?' 'No, ma'am, I'm only passing through.' But I couldn't help asking her how such little children managed to throw stones so accurately and so furiously. 'They're not children. Mine is already thirty. Can you see him? The one with his mouth open who is tying the string to the stone.' 'That's impossible, he's a miniature.' The woman told me that her neighbour's child was fifty. Then I commented, at the risk of seeming rude, that the children must be stunted. 'They're the children of abandoned women; if they grew we would no longer be abandoned.' 'Why were you abandoned?' She told me that almost all of them had a husband who had gone to war: some of them had died, others had stayed where they had fought even though the war had finished, and started a family. 'Everywhere,' she said, 'is full of wars and the menfolk are desperate to go to war.' Unable to contain my curiosity, I asked her: 'Do all the cocooned women here have a child?' 'Yes. Only one, the more to be pitied. If any more children are had, they dry up in the trunk of a tree, you see.' I couldn't help going on to ask, 'And can you ever leave the cocoon?' She answered with a sad look on her face that no, they could never leave the cocoon because it was the sign of them being abandoned. 'The thread is made of tears. One week the left eye spins it, the next week the right eye.' Then she shouted forcefully: 'Excuse me a moment, I'm going to eat!' The boy came out of the trunk, a lot calmer when he saw I was harmless, threw a stone up high, pulled on the string, and leaves fell to the ground. Picking one, he put it in his mother's mouth; she started to chew with such a beatific expression it made her look beautiful. Once she had eaten, she confessed: 'The leaf is both food and drink.' 'And what does your family say about all this?' 'I have no family, but it's worse for those who do, because they never come to visit them. Do you see? If the family did visit them they would no longer be abandoned women, and would have no reason to exist.' 'How long do you live?' 'That depends; if the leaf from the nutritious tree is from a good year, we can live until we are ninety … Some have lived to be a hundred.' A question had been tormenting me for some time, but I didn't know how to ask it, until it slipped out in spite of myself: 'How do you die?' 'The cocoon closes up, chokes us, and that's the end. I still have many years ahead of me if everything goes well. I've been cocooned for twenty-eight years now. When I was born there were only a few abandoned women. As happens everywhere, they have been multiplying. Now there are 486 of us.' Then she asked, cutting short her clear explanation: 'Would you like to eat a leaf?' I said thank you, but that I had just eaten a ham and cheese roll on the milestone by the nearby path. She called her son and told him that instead of standing there gaping he should do her the favour of eating something. And the small, shrunken boy inside the trunk began to chew his leaf. 'Before I leave, dear lady, tell me, when the cocoon closes up, what happens?' 'We roll.' With an expressive look she pointed to her right, where the wood ended in a ravine. 'At the bottom there's the Lake of Colourless Water. When the cocoon closes up, the boy or girl pushes it, and it rolls down.' I looked around me, thinking 'what a sad village', and couldn't help saying so out loud. 'That's not true, the cheese village is much worse. If you have time to listen to me for a while, I'll tell you what happens there.'

Journey to the Village of Cheeses, as told by the Cocooned Woman

There is not a single tree to be seen there. Everything is meadows and more meadows. And what grass! Radiant, quivering, always freshly growing, always enamelled with tiny flowers. The cows devour it by day, but at night it grows back. Everything that at nightfall was a bare field and nothing more, by first light is once again an emerald green. The cows produce milk once a month. Produce. I mean they really produce milk. No one milks them. The day they are due to do so, always on the fifteenth of the month, they weep endlessly from all their suffering. 'And couldn't someone help by milking them, even if it is just as they are about to release the milk?' That's impossible, because they are scalding. Their bowels prepare the cheese, and while it is being prepared and the cows are releasing the milk, they burn like an oven from muzzle to tail. When they think the milk in their bowels is thick enough, they release an intermittent stream from each udder, a thick stream that starts making a pie on the ground. Then they start turning in a slow circle so that the pie is nice and round. Once the wheel of cheese is complete, the pie fills with worms; whiter than the cows' stomachs. When someone comes to try and pick up the cheese they can't, because the worms have stuck it to the ground, and the cows charge again and again so that the worms can eat the cheese in peace. They are cheese worms. All they leave is the rind: golden and dark. Naturally, the inhabitants of the village are dying of hunger; if they want to eat they have to chew grass at the break of day. Occasionally some desperate person approaches the cheese, defying the danger of being charged by the cows, and if they are lucky may even manage to tear off a piece of rind. They chew it moving their whole head up and down, because it is harder than stones. No need to tell you that the inhabitants of this cursed village are little more than skin and bone and can hardly walk, so great is the weakness consuming them. They all take on the colour of the cheese rinds and, when they die, the living use the driest bones to light the stove. 'You see?' the cocooned woman told me serenely, 'how there is always someone worse off?'

Journey to the Village of Absolute Sorrow

This village was indeed different from the others. In it there was not even a garden, or a flower, not even the saddest of trees. Every street without exception was cobbled; all the houses were made of stone. In the high windows – inside the houses they had to use stepladders to close them – there was no glass, only shutters which as night fell shut with a latch. The inhabitants made a living from selling stone to the other villages because in that region there were quarries to spare. Red stone, with veins a darker red, the red of coagulated blood; it was as though the veins were speaking, because they traced arabesques. As with clouds, in them you could see or imagine animals: birds, fish, wild boars, a deer or two, frightened rabbits, stinking foxes, wild rats, stoical marquineldes, and the occasional startled owl ... stones possibly born of some earthquake, piled up, perhaps spat out in horrifying blocks by a volcano extinguished over the centuries. The villagers didn't look; they walked about unsteadily, with their heads down. In the square I reached, a crowd of people were weeping. Long drops fell from their eyes, sliding down their cheeks and chests. They were crying, it seems, for those who started wars, for the murdered, for all the injustices, for the crippled, for deprived parents, for all the many birds caught in snares, for all the hunted deer, for the rivers that burst their banks, for the barren fields, for the storms that swept everything away, for the ruined harvests, and because the mountains of stone surrounding the village didn't allow them to see the sun either at the moment of birth or at the moment of death.

Journey to the Village of Well-Bred Rats

It was a village much like any other. Flowers at the windows; even flowers on the flat roofs . . . and complete silence, as if no one lived there. In the middle of a shady street I jumped as over my feet ran a rat the size of a rabbit. She stopped a bit further on, turned to me and shouted from a distance: 'Sir, sir! Would you let me nibble on a house?' I didn't know what to say; I could only look at the rat who was looking at me with red eyes, her head bent forwards. Then, between my feet, a small rat appeared, then another, and another, seven altogether. They joined the big rat and all began to sing: 'Why don't you say yes, why don't you say yes . . .' I looked down, and they must have thought I was agreeing, because they dashed towards an old house and started gnawing at its base, snip snip, crunch crunch, over and over. When they had had enough, they wiped their little snouts with their front paws, looked at me again, and strolled away up the street. A man came out from the house they had been gnawing, trousers in tatters and his ears torn. 'Please, come in,' he said in a faint voice, 'have a seat.' We sat by the window. The flowers on the sill were petunias. 'This village,' he began, 'is unlike any other village. As you have probably noticed, the houses are made of wood, from the foundations to the roofs. Every ten or twelve years there's nothing left of the village. If we had stones nearby perhaps we would build houses with them, but the quarry is 234 kilometres away, and we are all too disheartened to undertake the adventure of collecting them . . . besides, there was once a determined man, or perhaps one simply less aware than the others, who went with his cart to collect stones and build a house that would last a lifetime. He had a wife and four children. Four boys. Handsome, tall boys . . . The finest flowers of child-hood. One day, I can't remember if it was Christmas Day or New Year's Eve, everyone in the house vanished. Neither parents nor children were anywhere to be seen. The rats hadn't left so much as their bones. They were teaching us a hard lesson. So we carried on building the houses of wood, as much out of weariness than as a precaution. What if all of us, absolutely all of us, were to build stone houses, would we be saved? We were never courageous enough. We have to build them out of wood so that the rats can gnaw at them and be satisfied, and above all so that they allow the people of the village to remain alive. Once, we prominent men in the village met together in the Ginebrera wood to discuss the matter. We were trying to fool the rats: to make the foundations of the houses – at least the foundations – out of stone. Whatever the cost in health or hard work. They must have been spying on us, because the next morning all of us who had been at the meeting, and only us, woke up to find our ears had been half-eaten. All of our earlobes, on the scrap heap. As I told you, every ten years the village is razed, and there's nothing else for it than to start building a new one. A little further this way, a little further that way. Come with me.' We left the house and he had me follow him up the street. At the top there was a viewing platform, and from there the man, as sad as the saddest person I have ever met, stretched out his arm and pointed down into the valley. I could see a real swarm of men sawing, smoothing, piling up planks and hauling trees. 'We could all be rich, because the earth of this land is fertile and everything grows, but we have to waste time building houses instead of sowing and harvesting!' I jumped. We were surrounded by rats who were listening to what we were saying. When the man saw what was happening, he explained to them: 'We'll make a village for you out of the sweetest, softest wood.' 'Thank you, thank you . . .' all the rats squeaked in unison. One very pretty rat shouted: 'We're hungry and want to eat, always, always.' 'Do eat,' said the man, his eyes lifeless, his voice faint. All the rats set upon two of the prettiest houses and immediately there came the noise of their crunch crunch. When I saw how busy they were I whispered in the man's ear, which was so badly chewed it hung like a festoon: 'Why don't you kill them?' He looked at me pityingly: 'Everything you care to suggest as a solution has been tried for twelve hundred years. It's as if death multiplied them just in order to punish us.' I heard a voice squeaking at my feet: 'Naughty! Naughty!' I looked down and saw a nice-looking rat beginning to gnaw at my trousers. I'm still running.

Journey to the Village of Witchcraft

'I suggest you go to the village down there, can you see it?' The view is blocked by the trees, but it's right behind them, come on! Can't you see it, obscured by the foliage?' This is what an ageless woman said to me, dressed all in black, her ample skirts gathered at the waist. Her round face framed by a scarf neatly tied under her chin. 'You'll fall in love with it.' And she gave a half smile.

The day was ending by the time I reached the village, a village more or less the same as any other, with low one-storey houses, two-storey at most; streets, some narrow, some wide; a square with arcades; a watering-trough; an inn; all kinds of shops and an undertaker. I strolled round the village, went everywhere in it, and thought the woman's idealised view of this completely boring village must stem from nostalgic childhood memories. I left it slowly, my thoughts lingering on the people living there. They looked like normal people yet something in their eyes was disturbing. Not very disturbing, only a little. As if suddenly they were fleeing from where they were and embarking on an interior journey, a long way inside them-selves, beyond space. I sat halfway up a slope, right next to a spring. As it was a gentle evening and I was quite tired,

I thought I would like to see the moon rise from beside that spring which softly sang its song of water escaping from deep dungeons.

Night was drawing in. Lights came on in the village. But the darkness seemed filled with the tales of trees born in a certain place thanks to a very firm determination, and of grass sown by a very wise hand in places where it could grow greener. Soon not a single light was left on in the village, they had all gone out at once, and the glow descending from the sky was not the usual glow, but one with blue stripes. And suddenly, on a lightning-coloured stripe as wide as a narrow track, I saw the first completely naked person floating on that illuminated ray, just as if they were lying in bed and pulling the sheets to their chin, even though there were none. Out of the darkness another person appeared, floating into the light, followed by another and another, more and more of them. Some were lying face down, their arms outstretched as though under a pillow, others with their hands behind their head, others on their side with their legs drawn up, others twisted, others flat on their backs with arms and legs spreadeagled, and many newborn babies, probably all the newborn babies in that village, floating in mid-air and moving their lips as if they were sucking on star milk. A little girl sitting in the empty sky rubbing her eyes before lying down on the light, covering her legs with a non-existent sheet . . . and all this was so natural, so extraordinarily commonplace, so real, that it was not until I had gazed at the entire line of sleeping people that I realised the village had disappeared: the houses, the trough, the inn, the square and its arcades, none of them were anywhere to be seen. All at once a sliver of moon appeared, the wind picked up, and all the space between me and the sleepers was filled with thistledown. Once it had passed, without my noticing the change, as if someone extremely powerful had transported me, I found myself not beside the melodious spring, but on the shore of a lead-coloured lake which reflected in itself the mysterious sliver of moon, glancing at me out of the corner of its eye and with a half smile like the woman in black who had told me that the village – can't you see it beyond the foliage? – was the prettiest village in the world.

Journey to the Village of Knitting Grandmothers

In summer they are put in an enclosure under a pergola covered by a black vine. In winter they are placed in a glass shed heated by three oil stoves. The benches they sit on have the softest wool cushions on them, covered in striped cretonne. The grandmothers work all year round. They enter the enclosure at seven in the morning and the shed in winter at eight, also in the morning. In both summer and winter they leave their work of knitting at nightfall. When they go to work they carry with them baskets packed with balls of wool and of every colour of cotton, as well as knitting needles of various sizes. They are taken food on varnished oak trays, food generally consisting of vegetables, pork chops, fried fish, chicken with pepper, mulled chocolate for their afternoon snack, splendid mugs of milky coffee and bread and butter rolls for breakfast. They are very well fed. They are hard-working, and spend the hours counting: one, two, purl one. A stitch to the right, one back, three to the right, purl one. They never stop. They make the sheets of white cotton, and so too the pillow slips. Blankets are knitted with two strands of different-coloured wool, for example green and pink, magenta and blue. Men's trousers are always grey wool. Their waistcoats are wine-coloured. The socks, black. Skirts are all chocolate-coloured, because it is a colour that doesn't show the dirt. Nappies are, as is well-known, pink cotton for girls, sky-blue cotton for boys. The grandmothers also knit towels, napkins. Tablecloths too – but these give them a lot of trouble because they make them multicoloured and have to change their balls time and again. They also knit rugs, and so that they don't crumple, their daughters and daughters-in-law put broad strips of strong card under them. The grandmothers never stop. Sometimes, not always, they tell one another stories: about the fire-eater; about the man who called down the lightning and when the lightning came it said it didn't want to kill him because he wasn't worthy of dying by fire; about the woman who was constantly sweeping her house, the veranda, and even the kitchen garden, with a heather broom; about the girl born with two knitting needles drawn on her pupils. They laugh a lot, but softly. They don't lift their eyes from their work, even though they know how to knit without looking at the needles and almost without counting the stitches, they are so experienced. The grandmothers all look alike: white hair combed back, with a bun on the back of the head, spectacles halfway up their nose, mouths with thin lips, and such tiny feet from never having to walk that they knit themselves slippers with felt soles so that the bottom of their feet won't get hurt. When you pass by the enclosure or the shed, the click-clack of the knitting needles gladdens the heart. When the eldest grandmother dies, she is immediately replaced by a younger one and is buried without sorrow. On her tomb – all the tombs face the rising sun – they leave a crown of coronindus and a bouquet of shiny metal knitting needles. So that it lasts.

Journey to the Village of the Two Roses

The village had been built on the flat top of a lonely mountain rising out of a sea of wheat fields. It was small: twelve houses and an inn. The mountain wasn't very high. Its western slope was a burrow for hares and rabbits. On its eastern slope the vegetation was exuberant. On its western slope it never rained. On its eastern slope it never stopped. And on the rainy side there were twelve springs: one of lavender, one of rosemary, one of watercress, one of camomile, one of the lizard, one of the partridge, one of the scorpion, one of the ant, one of the swallow, one of the sparrowhawk, one of the dove, one of the nightingale, one of the finch . . . not twelve, thirteen. The houses were all farmhouses, with sloping roofs, haylofts, wells, threshing floors, cellars. On the mountain top wheat grew, sprouted, turned green and then golden; it was the best and most renowned in all the region. Every ear a tiny loaf of bread. The village's inhabitants had no wish to know the future. They had never been in touch with the dead nor had they ever had the lines of their hands read, never read the cards. They had no need to. Because when the family was to expect good news, on a wall in their house, the dining-room wall opposite the hearth, there appeared a big blue rose the size of the palm of a hand, its blue petals made up of many different shades of blue, a blue of great wisdom. The rose appeared just as the sun does, that is, she appeared at the bottom of the wall and climbed little by little until, a handspan before reaching the ceiling, she fell still as if she was asleep. Half eclipsed, half asleep, she stayed in the house for a night and a day to make sure she was seen. Then she vanished without a trace. And when the family was about to receive bad news, such as the death of a child or a relative, or the threat of a poor harvest, or a sick sheep or goat or cow or horse or hen or dove or suckling pig, there appeared, again on the dining-room wall, the one opposite the hearth, as the reader has already supposed, a black rose, a rose of a varnished, shiny black colour: made of porcelain. Using a special tool so as not to break or damage her, they carefully pulled her from the wall and kept her in the top drawer of the sideboard, as a reminder of great sorrow.

Journey to the Village of Lazy Men

I came up against a riverbank crowded with small boats. All of a sudden I heard a voice, almost above my head, ringing like a bell.

'Listen traveller: in this village newborn children never stop. From the day they're born, they can stand up straight, and on the third they run hither and thither tearing up grasses, piling up dead leaves, putting them in sacks. They are always born in autumn. From the age of five they go into the wood to chop down trees and drag the trunks to the outskirts of the village, with the older children helping them. They saw the trunks lengthwise and pile them up. From ten onwards they begin building boats; but at twenty-five, not a day earlier or later, they stop moving. Stretched out on the ground, they get in everyone's way. Soon they are very carefully taken to the riverbank, where they are put into boats, then moored to the trunk of a poplar, where they live lulled by the incessant lapping of the water. The youngest serve them food: for lunch and dinner a plant sprout from the woolly grass, tender as an asparagus tip with a taste like grilled meat. They chew as if chewing on rubber, and spend their days staring at the changing light, the mirror of the waters cradling them, the passing clouds shaped like sheep that always become rosy at dusk, the falling leaves, the stars that before they depart with the night shout their joy as one. They sleep whenever they want to, wake up when their sleep is done and, if they so wish, laugh a little when the rain caresses their faces. They die without a word, and their bodies quickly dry out. The youngsters untie the boat of the man who has just died, and off goes the boat and bones, drifting downstream.

'Although there are only men in the village, the survival of the race is not a problem. At age thirteen every youth, suffering and sweating, produces a black worm. After a fortnight, out of the worm appears a small animal with thirty legs that little by little – it takes a year – turns into a clever, healthy being, as sly as anything. That's it. Full stop. Hurry on your way, traveller. Higher up you'll come to a footbridge.'

Journey to the Village of the Dead

The village doesn't exist. The war destroyed it and no one bothered to rebuild it. It is close by a river lined with poplars and a little-used path with cart-tracks half erased over time. At midnight, once at the end of June and again at the end of December, every year, the path fills with a procession of the dead. They wait until the moon is high so that the river reflects them and acts as their guide. Their clothes hang off them; many of them have their shrouds trailing along the ground. They pass by, tall and sleepy. They can't hold up their heads: some have them slipped onto their left shoulder; others on the right shoulder; some have left them in the grave because when they rose their heads fell off, and so they have to go back to find them; others drop them in the fields and have to stoop to pick them up; a few carry them, arms outstretched, on the palms of their hands, charging at the shadows. They don't sing. They don't laugh. They are silent. They walk towards the village that had been theirs and spend hours entranced by the places where once they had houses, kitchen gardens that they dug, where they had a shed always full of hoes and mattocks, stables warm from the breathing of horses and cows, fields of wheat and barley, groves of almonds and olives, wells of always-fresh cool water, the spring at the foot of the chestnut mountain. They had been shot in the centre of the threshing floor, and all that spilt blood still cries out for mercy . . . the cry of the owl accompanies them, and if they had tears, they would sometimes weep. The cemetery is old, the tombs and niches damaged by the passage of time, with its rains, frosts, armies of ants . . . worn stones, tombs lifted by the fury of roots, cypresses punished by the buffeting wind, drilling the sky. Before the first light of day they leave the village in their baggy clothing, half-naked in their shrouds; heads swaying; erect and sorrowful they return to the cemetery down paths impossible to discern beneath the thick weeds no one cuts down. They go back to their resting places along the poplar path, along the path of madder, the path of sweet yarrow, the path of white nettle, the path of St John's wort, the path of red grass, the path of snail grass, the path of canon's grass, the path of grass of the innocents, the path of grass of strange disease, the path of grass of the breathless, the path of grass of Sant Pelegrí, the path of the grass of the traitor, duplicated in the water as the dying moon casts their reflections, allowing them to think they are still alive among reedbeds and purslane, always waiting for the arrival of the solstices which means it is time for them to come out for a stroll.

Journey to the Village of Glass

Absolutely everything was glass, starting with things usually made of wood, for example: walls and roofs, interior and exterior doors, as well as the streets, the pavements, the church and its bell tower, the bells, the clappers, the headstones in the cemetery, the coffins, the tombs – so that if it interests you, you can follow the process of decomposition of the human body – and the benches and fences in public and private gardens, all the furniture in a flat, a villa, a mansion. The eagle monument was a big leafless glass tree, with seven eagles, wings spread, on its branches. The monument to the moon consisted of a huge glass ball sculpted with craters and spectacular mountains. The inhabitants of the village don't have to possess books – they know how to find in the air, engraved for eternity, all that has happened in the world, all that is going to happen, all that the flames destroyed in the library of Alexandria. The wisdom of the world is theirs. I was very astonished there was nothing that couldn't be seen, and this nothing that couldn't be seen means the everyday life of people. Marvellously beautiful people, their bodies well proportioned, without a blemish, their fingernails as perfect as half a dove's egg, their hair unusually long, their eyes totally transparent, with an angelic expression. Reserved and affable, their minds clear ... In short, a people both physically and intellectually superior, possessing great attraction, powerful and fearsome. These glassed-in people reach incredible ages. Naturally they live in sight of everyone, and this means they have to control their bad moods, rages, fury, envy, hatred, the desire – in the most extreme of them – to kill ... and by dint of hiding their evil, their confessable and their shady instincts, of stifling their perverse passions, they eventually no longer have them. Monotony? I don't know. What I do know is that everybody is of extreme purity. The only spectacle they don't allow to be seen in full is the spectacle of love-making, which they perform behind thick glass walls that veil the details, because it is the detail that counts. Even so, or rather despite this, you can see what is going on and you can admire the levels of sublimation they reach in the most elated moments of the sexual, let's call it romantic, adventure. You can watch them eat; they eat as if they weren't doing so, and the expression on their faces, no matter how hungry they are when they sit at the table, is never bestial, just as their faces – or what you can glimpse of their faces – are not when they die in the pleasure of love. I never saw them preoccupied, never with knitted brows – their foreheads are high and smooth, their eyes never flashing with anger, even when some creature of the night destroys the flowers in their garden, all of them made of glass. This is the village that left me the fondest memory. 'Why, if you fell in love with it, did you not settle there?' 'Because my task is not to stop but to carry on for ever; to continue the endless hunt for dark hearts and unknown traditions.'

Journey to the Village of Rivers Without Water

They summon a dowser and tell him, 'Search for water.' And the dowser who has arrived with his divining rod begins the ritual. Up and down, round and round, until he comes to a sudden halt; the rod shows signs of life, that is, of water, and so then, to celebrate, the mayor invites the dowser to eat *homard à la américaine* in any village on the coast, then brings in men to dig and they all start the exhausting task of freeing the water from the layer of earth covering it without drowning it, because it is well known that water needs its paths. Suddenly, the river appears in spectacular fashion. As soon as it is uncovered it gushes into the air, so that everyone is as soaked as a fish. It is never a wide, raging river, only a puny one, but with a deep bottom. A man from the village, a first cousin of the gravedigger, told me: 'The village, the whole village, do you see, is sighing for a river. A river with banks full of reeds and rushes, broad banks lined with poplars, a river you can sail barges on, with sailors shouting on deck as they trade in spices and cereals. A romantic river full of ancient history, with every so often a rocky castle and a damsel at the topmost window waving a silk handkerchief to encourage the most besotted navigator to embark on the adventure of love. A river that wants to live with us all our lives and those of our heirs, because the tragedy of our village is that once discovered, the river does not last. One fateful day, just when the village is beginning to live a happy life, tranquil and trusting because the flow of water fully supplies all its needs, the water dries up. So then, back to work again; the dowser is summoned, the mayor invites him to the Lady Penguin inn, men are brought in to dig, water is discovered, a jet of water spurts into the air, dams here and there, streams diverted to the kitchen gardens, and everyone planting fruit trees ... Come with me ...' He took me by the arm and I didn't protest even though I don't like people being familiar with me, and led me to the top of an average sized mountain – about three hundred metres high – from where you could see the village and its surroundings. At our feet lay the valley; it was covered with roads. He told me: 'They're made of sand, with the occasional scraggy tree or dried-out reed in the middle. Do you see what I was saying? All these sandy roads were once rivers; now they are only the spectre of rivers. Not a single drop of water flows along them. Don't tell me it isn't enough to make you tear your hair out.' On the western side, in an area free of dead rivers, a man dressed all in black who looked small in the distance, balancing a divining rod in front of him in a state of utter concentration, surrounded by anxious onlookers, was asking the earth where it was hiding, in what unknown depths it was hiding, the fertilising water that would allow the good people to live from pears and peaches, grapes and plums, cabbages and aubergines, lettuce and escarole, peppers and broccoli, green beans, saffron and cumin . . .

Journey to the Village of Hanged Men

I had slept deeply in a very beautiful valley filled with grass dotted with white and yellow flowers that looked like miniature daisies, even though they weren't. A light breeze bent them. On the far side of a thick expanse of reeds, which cost me a great deal of trouble and effort to cross, I came to a sudden halt in front of a wood as gloomy as a cathedral. Dangling from each oak tree – or perhaps they were holm oaks – was a hanged man, dressed in a white shirt, and a pair of trousers and waistcoat made from fawn calfskin speckled a lighter brown. I turned my head so as not to dwell on such a sad spectacle and, worried I might trip, I walked quickly to the village with its freshly whitewashed houses and recently swept and watered streets. A man with a very short neck and ferret-like eyes almost bumped into me, 'Sorry, I wasn't looking.' On his back he was carrying a coil of rope. In the doorway of the house he had just left, a beautiful young woman, a child in her arms, was staring after him. When I drew near her, she said good-day and I couldn't help asking, pointing to the man who had just turned the corner, 'Where is he going?' The woman ran her fine fingers through the child's hair and said in a low voice: 'To hang himself.' Sad for both the woman and the child – she was about to lose a husband, the child a father – I couldn't help asking her another question: 'Why?' From a house further up the street emerged another short-necked man, also with a coil of rope on his back. Like the first one, as well as the rope, he was also wearing an immaculately white shirt, and trousers and waistcoat of fawn calfskin speckled a lighter brown . . . 'You're not from this village.' I explained I was bored at home because people went round and round the streets endlessly shouting 'Freedom! Freedom!' and that I'd set out to see the world, meaning that for the moment I had no home. 'Ah,' said the woman, coming closer, 'so you can't know that in this village all the men are sinners. The moment they're born they have sin stuck to their palate. As soon as boys become men they live only to have a wife and children. Every man wants sixteen children. And he enjoys producing them so much that eventually he is punished; the children die on them, two by two, until they are left with one of each: a boy and a girl, and madness begins to grow in the line of the man's brain dividing the two halves, so that all they want to do is hang themselves. Old folk explain that the two surviving children are the ones who were conceived roughly, amid scratches, as if it was a duty. And the ones made with care, in the moonlight on soft grass . . . have you seen the valley of little white flowers? They are the ones whose thread is cut with a single sweep of death's scythe.' I soon baptised her as the singsong woman, because she spoke as if she were singing. 'Do you know something? They conceive the children at night, smartly dressed and with eyes wide open surveying the darkness . . .' 'But,' I told her, 'if they weren't made, that would be the end of the village.' 'Of course,' said the woman, putting a red handkerchief over the face of the child, who had fallen asleep. 'But is it worth the trouble to keep it going? Where does that get us? Look, life here means planting cabbages, beans, chickpeas, carrots and aubergines. Raising chickens, collecting their eggs, breaking them, making omelettes . . . and being thankful the hens don't get sick and die, and chopping wood and cooking everything together – you see what I mean – and giving birth. While the woman gives birth to the first ten children, the man dances. Even so, it's as if with the first child that's born, he regrets having done so. But he can't avoid going on. He can face the second one and the third and fourth, if he is strong enough. But by the sixth, at most, he doesn't know what to do with his life. The woman feels him shrinking, shrinking . . . and he spends his days lost in thought. By the fifteenth, and above all the sixteenth, it's as if he has gone mad from all the births and deaths he has had to witness, and he starts plaiting the rope. He kills the calf; uses its skin to make trousers and waistcoat, neat in a white shirt he goes into the wood, chooses a tree, makes sure the branch is strong enough, places the rope round his neck after making a slip knot, climbs onto a rock, and jumps. He swings peacefully forever. If you crossed the wood, you can't have failed to notice the look of happiness all the hanged men have.'

39

Journey to the Village of the Rainbow

Wandering here and there, up hill and down dale, I forded two rivers and suddenly, above a low mist, I saw stretching across the sky a rainbow so clearly outlined and of such amazing and distinct colours I had to pause in wonder to study it. I walked towards this marvel until I found myself in a field of flax. Many people, most of them women, with big baskets beside them, were picking it. They were wearing dresses down to the ground, striped horizontally with all the colours of the rainbow. The sight took my breath away. Some of the women saw me, straightened up, and with an arm in the air and smiling from ear to ear, they shouted a greeting: 'The deluge is over! The deluge is over!' I raised my arm as well, and half-laughing, asked the woman nearest to me: 'Is the deluge over, and will it not rain again?' She began to laugh; her teeth were multi-coloured, but her lips were pale. 'No, look, that's our cry of joy ... Do you see? The mist keeps the earth moist, and see how the flax grows.' The sun was coming out very pale, very shy, very slowly. A throng of women gathered round a young girl who was groaning. The woman who had spoken to me said the young girl was about to give birth, and did I want to see it ... 'Thanks, but I'd prefer to carry on.' But, against my wishes, I found myself pushed up close to the circle of onlookers and, when I was right there, a woman gave a cry and held up, against the sun, a baby as blond as an angel, the entire body striped horizontally with the colours of the rainbow. I must have looked very surprised because the woman holding up the baby told me: 'The colours will fade, and sixty days from now there will only be a pink line round the waist because it is a boy. Pink for a boy, violet for a girl.' 'Go to the village and they'll give you breakfast.' 'I'm not very hungry.' 'No matter; even the most reluctant eat our pastries in one gulp. They can never get enough of them.' All my life I've remembered that field of flax, and perhaps at the hour of my death I shall still see it covered in yellow, blue, red. At the entrance to the village there were three rows of men weaving. And behind them, three rows of women using a reed to stir colours in big pots. The colour of each pot corresponded to the colour of the paint in it, paint that another three rows of women were sprinkling on woven linen stretched out on boards. To my right, on big racks, the freshly painted cloths were drying in the sun. Without even realising where I was, I found myself in the middle of the village square. On tables of bare wood, surprisingly without any colour, were stacks of rectangular, brightly coloured pastries. And behind each table, a pretty girl was offering them. 'The sweetest, the best baked ... with a golden crust! Do you want them hot, or cold?' After leaving my bundle on the ground, I timidly took one.

Before biting into the pastry, I smelled it. Pure honey. The smell of forest honey. I couldn't explain it. I ate six that were so light it was as if I had only eaten one. 'How do you make them?' 'Semolina and tapioca. Before we put them in the oven we paint them, and when they come out we give them a second coat. Can you see the pots? And the paintbrushes?' The brushes were small, their handles striped with horizontal stripes like those on the young and old women's dresses from this village that always, always had the rainbow above it. Suddenly, from every door of the houses around the square, emerged men, women and children waving multicoloured streamers and shouting at the top of their lungs: 'Glory be!' The women came in from the flax field. In front was the young girl who had given birth: she was holding the baby up so that everyone could see him. It pained me to leave that village, and when I was quite far away I could still hear them singing: 'The deluge is over! The deluge is over!' And the rainbow trembled, collapsing on the earth with one foot on either side and its back touching the sky.

Journey to the Village of Snails and Mud

I was accompanied there by a man who was the carpenter from the next village. Before we arrived, he warned me: 'You sir, who have visited so many villages, I'm sure you haven't ever come across one like this.' Not a house was to be seen. Nothing was to be seen. We stopped by the edge of a low wall that went round in a big, big circle. At the foot of the outside of the wall were soft patches of tender grass and more and more bushes of fennel. The grass and the fennel were covered in land snails. And all the inside of the wall was filled with the shapes of men and women covered in mud. 'They roll naked in the mud, completely bare. Can you see their heads? They're so big that's the only thing the mud cannot cover.' Above the closed circle of the wall, probably so that the mud could not spread, hung a cloud that was neither too white nor too grey. Further off, right in the centre of the big circle, rose a hill with gentle slopes but not a blade of vegetation. My companion said: 'You see? When they want to get the mud off, in the same way that in the other villages people sunbathe, the villagers here climb the hill suffering and sweating, and I say suffering and sweating because they slide down all the time, and at the top they bathe in the rain. But they soon come down again; they like living face down in the mud too much, they play games in it, throw handfuls at each other's heads and faces. They're happy that way.' 'What do they live on?' 'Snails. They eat them, horns and all, alive and unpurged.' 'And how do they die?' 'They never die; the mud preserves them and the snail meat makes their skins slimy. If you could see one of them up close, if one would like to show you and came out of the mud, you'd see the skin covering them is the tightest in the world.' 'And when the cloud leaves, how do they wash?' 'The cloud never leaves. It has permanently rented that piece of sky. It's always above them, and always drizzling. When the men and women stretched out on top of the hill are tired of being clean and seeing their skin, they let themselves slide back down into the mud, which is in fact where they live.' 'Amazing . . .' I said.

Journey to the Village of the Thirty Young Girls

The village, as pretty as a picture, was abandoned. All the houses were the same, and they were all surrounded by a garden. Gardens with bushy, wild, blossoming plants because it was a region with heavy rainfall. The houses were built in a round fringed by giant acacias, leaves facing the sky, flowers carpeting the ground and perfuming it with the smell of honey. In the centre of the square was the cat cemetery. Each tombstone had the name of the cat buried there engraved on it, and a portrait of the animal, behind glass and with a gilded frame, was hanging from the stela. The portrait only showed the little head. Round heads, with eager whiskers, innocent, thoughtful eyes, and stiff, alert ears. On the gravestone, no, I think it was below the portrait, figured the name of the creature, its date of birth and of its death. At first I was surprised by the names of the cats: SPARROWER, NIGHTINGALER, GREENFINCHER, GOLDFINCHER and so on. The tombstones were all made from the stone known as 'partridge's eye' because it is a pale grey colour, speckled with a dark grey that is almost black. It apparently came from the quarry in the neighbouring village where all the men, without exception, were stone cutters and offered the stone to other villages, and even to some towns. They were strong men, with big feet to be able to sleep upright, and hands with short, thick fingernails cut right back to the quick. One of them passing by – I don't know where he was heading or where he had come from, and I didn't think to ask – stopped when he saw me looking at the deserted village and the cat cemetery in the middle of the round square. 'It's a shame . . . but what can you do. Life is full of surprises . . .' He extended his arm to point at the surrounding gardens and houses. 'It was the prettiest village in the world; there has not been and will not be another one like it anywhere else. Thirty young girls lived in it . . . that's right, there were thirty of them. All of them on their own, all of them blonde, all tall and slender, with small hands and feet. Each in their own little house. Can you see the houses? All of them with a sloping roof, all the roofs forming one long slope, all with barred windows, the iron of the bars making a frame, all of them with luxury curtains: gauze as fluffy as a pink twilight when the pink at twilight turns to lilac. In the dining-room, Pakistani rugs, impeccable white furniture, sofas with little cushions in front of the hearth, lazy armchairs on each side of the sofa, little crystal tables, or better, rock crystal of the sort that looks like frozen water with aniseed. Mantelpiece decorated with a white jug and a wildflower inserted in it. A bird cage with a porcelain bird in it, the mouth always open. White walls with no pictures but here and there a blonde ear of wheat drawn by hand. The bedroom furniture, it goes without saying, also white. Single beds, a wide, low wardrobe, a squat bedside table, a snow-white dressing table: everything as white as foam on a wave. Houses, as you can see from what I'm explaining, of women in love with everything that was theirs. The kitchen, white tiles from floor to ceiling, decorated with hanging utensils, all made of copper: ladles, pots and pans. And a frying pan or two.' All of a sudden, the man who was so keen to talk raised his arm furiously and waved it round his head: 'Can you see the square? Acacias. An immaculate flower. Can you hear the birds? Perhaps you didn't notice, but behind the houses lies a wood of ancient holm oaks and plane trees as old as the world, with proud trunks. Trees like no others because they are so leafy, so full of birds.' The sun had not yet risen. On the side where it would come up the sky was turning purple and the birdsong was becoming increasingly deafening, increasingly joyful. A song that was more than happy, one that was victorious. 'Can you hear it? And it's the same every day. They sing as if they were singing to the glory of God. They have been the winners, of course, because the young girls were so delicate they lived only on the birds their cats caught. Trained cats, skilled at catching their feathered prey . . . cats that, at the right moment, the girls castrated so that they wouldn't be distracted from their hunting by all that nonsense of love and the moon, of rooftops and becoming fathers. As you can see, the name of each cat corresponded to the name of the bird they most liked to catch. You saw it, didn't you? The headstones in the cemetery? Goldfincher, hunter of goldfinches. Sparrower, hunter of sparrows. Greenfincher, hunter of greenfinches ... The thirty young girls didn't have any offspring either, not because of a snip of the scissors, but because that's how they were. The years went by for them, their faces became wrinkled, their hair turned white and as is natural, it all came to an end for both girls and cats, what can you do? But, hand on heart, I have to confess that the village is still absolutely beautiful. Look at it, now the rising sun is striking it.'

Journey to the Village of Fear

The village is sensational. The houses stand at a distance from one another, built on top of a low mountain, where simply by moving your eyes you can see the sea and the white crest of the Pyrenees. They are cheerful houses, open to the four winds, all two hundred square metres, with big openings: a lot of glass and few bricks. Their bathroom walls are covered from floor to ceiling with floral mosaics, always of roses. Some are of pink roses, some of blue roses, others of yellow. The main room has a hearth with the chimney piece in a beam of oak, built on a wall of reddish stone – with leaden streaks – of a rust colour. Windows and balconies open onto the garden. A garden of a hundred thousand square metres. When they bought the land for their marvellous shelters to be constructed on, the villa owners found it already wooded. There are mimosas of the kind gardeners call 'everlasting', others that when in bloom, which is always in the month of February, look like a cluster of golden balls; others that do not flower much but grow quickly to dizzying heights, right up to the sky. There is a path lined with mulberry trees whose broad leaves are a crystalline green. There are linden trees that are not as fine as those of Schönbrunn but still quite something. An olive tree with three branches, the sign of peace, presides over the entrance, alongside three cypresses that are the sign of a warm welcome. Gathered together there are a dozen poplars, the underside of their wavy leaves shining like silver, half a dozen maples, a horse chestnut, two firs, three pines that cast a little shade on the barbecue, a dozen Japanese flowering cherry trees with their heavy pink blossom, and for fruit trees, usually planted behind the houses, there are four apricots, six red plum trees, six peach trees, three cherry trees and four almond trees so that you can enjoy a display of beautiful white blossom at the height of winter. The only flower: the finest roses, like those on the mosaics in the bathrooms, blue, yellow and rose-coloured . . . and that's enough. There are innumerable shrubs: veronicas, buddleias, forsythias, cotoneasters, cinerarias, rosemary . . . Ah, I forgot to mention two weeping willows at the edge of the pond, three Judea trees, the tree of love. And among the fruit trees, a lemon tree. Although the tree that dominates the garden, even though they have cut down lots of them to make room for others, is the holm oak, a very boring but very reassuring tree: always strong, disease-free, its leafage is perennial, resisting all the attacks of the winds, it sprouts securely, its trunk is protected by a thick bark no longer sought after for corks, but that gives the tree the shelter it needs and which allows it, albeit very slowly, to live through the ages. But over this village of beautiful houses there hangs a sort of curse, a kind of unease that is poisonous and only shows itself at sunset and during the night ... Nothing ever happens, not a single unpleasant event has ever been mentioned, the village cannot be said to attract thieves, robbers, or people with reprehensible habits ... nothing of that kind. At day's end, the inhabitants of the houses rush to close windows and balconies, because they are overwhelmed by a profound feeling when they look at the moon or a cloud or the tops of the trees standing out against the cloudy or clear sky, that every leaf of every tree is an eye filled with power and intelligence, not looking at them but studying them and registering everything they are thinking. Why?

Journey to the Village of Gold

I soon saw the misshapen mountain, cleft down the middle, and at its foot, cart after cart, men and more men with picks and chisels, hammers and crowbars, men dotted about high up, impossibly balanced, on the verge of killing themselves, tied by the waist, arm, leg, or simply a foot to some life-saving ledge, digging and digging, excavating and excavating. The sun crashed into the mountain with its spider's web of paths so shiny they were blinding. Veins and more veins of gold. In this village they didn't do a lot with the gold; they put it, if one can say so, into their mouths. Before that they stacked it up everywhere and when they felt like it or thought they had excavated enough, they burnished it until it shone. This was their obsession; rub and rub, shine and shine, look how it shines, how it shines. As I said, they put it into their mouths: all of them had gold teeth, gold crowns on their teeth and molars. And the gravediggers constantly pulled from the corpses' mouths gold bridges, gold caps from teeth and molars before covering with sheets of gold the mother earth of the tombs where they buried the dead of that incredibly yellow and shiny village.

TRUE FLOWERS

Ballerina Flower

She is yellow and very dishevelled. Four tendrils emerge from her stem. She opens in mid-summer, at dawn with the sun. Her slender round petals are born in tiny pushes, and hang down. She gives off a perfume which combines the smell of woods – that is, dry – and mown grass – that is, damp. Once she has unfurled all her splendour, the tendrils spread, wrap round the nearest branches: they become as taut as wires. Captive, the flower begins the exhausting work of freeing herself. She slowly folds in on herself with little shakes, right and left. Forwards, back-wards. She tries, but when after a great deal of patience and grief she has only managed to become more entangled, she abandons her efforts. Begins to move in the opposite direction: she unfurls her dishevelled self, petals extended. When the impulse fades, she coils once more with an indomitable will, and just as rapidly uncoils, without knowing why. This struggle lasts for hours, and does not end until the stem breaks off at the tendrils and the flower droops. If some kindly soul passes by and notices this struggle starting – and has a pair of scissors with them – they cut the tendrils so that the flower can live in peace. If the passer-by is cruel, they leave things as they are, and even enjoy the spectacle.

Desperate Flower

Lives in marshes. With her root in the mud – she is of the nenuphar family – she would open prettily were it not for the centipede Xuribinga-Palangrin, which is born beneath the flower's calyx. Black, its feet mandarin-coloured, it lives in fear. Always with the fear that the Salamandril will appear. As soon as the centipede hears it approaching from afar – swooping down from the azure sky and the trembling light with the buzz of a blowfly – Xuribinga-Palangrin climbs the flower, squeezes her to prevent her opening, and if she is already half-open, forces her petals to close. A way of killing so as not to die. If the Salamandril gets to taste the flower, it lights up like a torch, attacks Xuribinga-Palangrin, and swallows it whole. Luckily the Salamandril has a trusting heart and is very innocent. If when it flies down it finds the flower closed and with

Xuribinga-Palangrin on top, the Salamandril returns to the azure and the trembling light. It soon dies, dry as a nail. And so does the flower. Dead before she can open, the victim of the fight for life of a poor stupid idiot.

Blue Flower
She is white and she is blue. That is, she is as white as a white rose, and suddenly turns blue. Apparently she is dyed by an insect, but no one knows how it does this. A moment's distraction, and she is blue. On one knee, sewn on with a thread of slime, the insect carries a small package, and inside this package, surrounded by eggs and by blue – pure induline – lies her mate. He sleeps all day and incubates the eggs, which fall into the package through a hole the insect has on its knee. When the time comes, the insect crawls into the very heart of the flower, drops the package, and the flower turns from white to blue, from top to bottom. They say – Oh, it's because her mate, when he sees himself wrapped in the flower, bursts the package and everything is flooded with blue juice – then the eggs appear, and soon the tiny insects fly off, each of them with a package on their knee. Be that as it may. But these are pure suppositions. The truth is that in the blink of an eye the white flower turns blue. How exactly? There's no way of knowing, and everyone is a little puzzled.

Magic Flower

Don't go! The Wood of Shattered Mirrors is a wood of pepper plants with leaves stained with evil. Every so often the wood is crossed by a cloud of white flies in a compact, drowsy flight. Don't go! The ground beneath the trees is littered with broken mirrors. As soon as you enter you go deaf. Don't go! Inside a hollow trunk lives the Magic Flower, surrounded by the eggs of the Bomb Ant, legs of the Violin Beetle, tears of the Face of Man. Mistress of her lair that is rotten with mushrooms and moss, she moves like flower and flame. A speck of dust ignites the grass and death comes from everything already dead. Each fragment of mirror is a fragment of life of each of the men who have left all they had in the wood. In each shard of mirror a fragment of those lives pulses brilliant, ardent, shimmering: three lines of rainwater, an undone collar, a hand still moving, part of a child, a handful of a doll's hair . . . In the shade of the green light, as you are trying to tie a fragment of life to its corresponding fragment of mirror, something stirs among the leaves . . . Bang! It has exploded on you, and before you hit the ground in pieces, your back is already covered with quicksilver. To act as a lure.

Red Flower

She is nailed to the branch, with no neck. Lit by a painful red, when the breeze turns to blow on her, the edges of her petals tremble. And at night, when the grass is cold and snakes drink milk, on every taut petal appears a drop of black blood: smooth and hard like the seeds of a watermelon. Damp. It's the sickness. Better not touch her. The sickness burns the flower and a shower of rain rots the sickness. Glow-worms, who are wise, light their lanterns. And look on.

Dead Flower
Somewhere in the world the Dead Flower is to be found. Covered in salt stars, time has dried her out, tall and empty, her leaves extended. A crazy springtime blew a seed on her, and the seed produced a plant, and the plant flowered with wretched flowers – a golden snowdrop, a honeyed foxglove or a yellow monkey flower, all of them consumed in the end by the salt stars. In the jumble of her roots the earth is grey, mixed with sand and pierced shells. From one leaf to another, the rain spider spins her web, weaving and weaving, night and day, tripping in the creases, yarning over, three stitches to the left, now a back loop, now a front loop, if the wind tangles it, I start again, and to make it thick I weave and weave, turn around, three chain stitches, it comes apart up above, has to be tied, I smooth out the sheet ... I weave the blanket and wait, mouth watering, for the blind moth with honeycomb wings that comes flying by ... The Dead Flower does not know when the spider is at work or when the little stars fall or come together. Nor does she know, shrouded in

the spider web, that the wild sea is watching over her, and sprinkling her with salt.

Happiness Flower

In a far-off land grows a wraithlike purple tree. It produces a flower as shiny as glass, rainbow-hued like glass, made of something very similar to a soap bubble. Neither the strange currents of love nor water on the verge of thirst – nothing in this world can compare to the pleasure offered by observing this flower, or to the moment when the setting sun makes her sing. She has to be looked at lying flat on the ground. Sometimes there are as many as ten people lying there, waiting with morbid desire, eyes frozen, for the flower to sing. The days are too white, the nights too dark . . . the sloping meadow ends in a cliff on the shore of a gulf. The flower sings and lulls them to sleep. Sleeping like stones, the men roll down and end up in the water where, after plummeting for 124 metres, they die open-mouthed, their teeth smashed. The fork-fish drills into their bodies and starts eating them from the inside.

Water Flower

She opens on the surface of the purest water in the world: that of the lakes, made from snow foam. She is small, ivory-white, like lemon balm. A drinking flower. Her petals become spoons, scoop up the water, and when they are full, quickly close up to form a bud so that the water doesn't spill, then they drink it. Afterwards they slowly open and rest. Once they are rested, they drink again. They do the same every night. When the blossom is over, the plant shrinks its stem and leaves its offspring, the flowers, alone with the water. All the benefit from so much drinking was for the plant. Nothing for the flowers. Only the hard work, a little coolness inside, and a blue cemetery.

Knight Flower

This flower is not a she. It's a he. Just as carnations, jasmines, wallflowers and yellow poppies are masculine in Catalan. Not to mention the Valencian jasmine of King Peter the Great, 'of big and wide flower'. The Knight Flower is always alert. At war with the wind. The Knight Flower is purple, with a saffron-coloured pistil. He opens in spring and does not wither until chestnuts ripen. His mission is to play the trumpet. The Knight Flower lives on the top of walls and keeps a lookout. The wind wants to smell all the flowers, to spread their perfume, and the Knight Flower warns the others. When the wind arrives, it finds them under lock and key. It is a very subtle war: a war of cunning. The wind hides, suddenly appears, disguises itself as a breeze, blows gusts at three hundred an hour. The Knight Flower, dressed in ecclesiastical purple, lord of the high walls, hears the wind coming and with his pistil trumpet: toot toot!... toot toot! 'Flowers shut!' The flower joyously commands. 'If you want to smell them, that's too bad, I won't let you strip their petals.'

Mean Flower

She is the colour of a mint sweet, full of different shades. She has one petal raised like a frill and two horizontal ones that emerge like two mussel shells, closed by a tuberous latch. This is a flower-mussel with a heraldic crest and a latch. If you stop to look at her, the crest waves angrily, the latch lifts up, the flower-mussel opens, and pokes out a little tongue as dark as chocolate, shiny as varnish. Furious at seeing a head on top of a man so close to her, she sticks out her tongue, mockingly.

Nameless Flower

As soon as she was born she loved everything: the piled-up aphid, the hidden worms sucking and sucking the damp earth, the lizard's tail, the rage of the bumblebee, the ants shooting out with a bundle on their head, the pelleted cockroach, the ladybird with a shell-jacket, the dragonfly about to wash its face, the dusty rain of the syringe flower. Everything. Every day she loved everything. Until the end of the long fine days brought the red wind, and the wind shook her violently and went off with one of her leaves. And another. And more. And she, in her tiny quiet voice, said to she didn't know whom: they are taking me away.

Each flying leaf was a letter. T.H.E.Y. ... the pause was a dot ... T.A.K.I.N.G. ... And no one heard her and the leaves rose and rose and, blowing hard, the wind jumbled them and that was that A.W.A. ....

Scattered Flower

In a bunch, as round as bullets, they smell of camphor and spend the whole day laughing. They shake from the morning until it grows dark. They fall into the river, sides splitting from laughing so much, and drift downstream with water chasing them and water carrying them away. A whirlpool halts them and they separate. Each one goes her own way – to the land of spiky feet, the land of the sewn-up mouth, the land of the nailed hand, the land of the trunk nose, to the land of eyes tight shut. And they all end up in the sea. Small bullets smelling of camphor, they roll and die laughing.

Tender Flower

Liquid and shaped like a grape – shall I fall or not through shady leaves? – she is born without being aware of it. The sky with its ball of fire, the sky with its ball of snow turns her into a pip, a cloudy white, the colour of water with aniseed. After three days alive she smells completely of blood. Shiny and slimy, a leech sucks at her eagerly and, once the flowering season is over, of all the delightful little grapes all that remain are little bundles of wrinkled skin: raisins.

Ceremonious Flower

Is nocturnal. When the Hidden Tailors sew the moon on the slope of the night, when the frog fills with wind, when the nightjar goes hunting, the Ceremonious Flower opens. During the day she sleeps, her petals are of gauze and fire red. She adorns. Is a flower for the bats flying round her, shadowy and innocent. Nosy. But even though for her the night has been one of keeping watch, and sleeping with the sun is such a delight for her, if she hears you nearby she cannot help opening: she pays a visit. Obviously, she doesn't say anything because she cannot talk, but she greets you courteously and doesn't leave you even for five minutes. She is the silliest of flowers.

Life Flower

Methuselah discovered her, put her in a flowerpot, put the pot in a cream-coloured bag sewn on his garment, and spent the empty hours looking at her in the shade of the cedar and the cypress, facing a field of lilies in delirium. He ate grape cakes. What a pleasure! But on one day of heavy clouds and a curtain of rain he slipped in a muddy pond, the pot broke, and Methuselah died aged three thousand and something, from watching the world

and the swallows go by. The flower went to find and give
life elsewhere. A generation goes by, a generation comes:
one turned towards madness, the other to common sense.
Everybody went around carrying a pot with the flower.
They met in Everyman Square and asked one another:
'What about yours?' 'She's blossomed seven times.' 'And
your father's?' 'And your brother's?' The flower lived protected, nourished by fine words and pure wisdom. Every
day there were more flowers. More people with lots of
life. People who were never sick. The years fell on them,
the years dropped away and they took the years on their
shoulders, on their noses if need be. Until one morning of
raging sun, when snakes stand erect, the doctors, chemists,
lawyers, married women, children wanting to inherit, all
met in secret ... They burned the flowers in the middle
of the square, smashed the pots, and it all ended up with
them queuing at the cemetery as there wasn't enough
earth to cover the old people with owl faces and worm-
eaten bones.

Black Flower
Seven wells and seven of the longest nights came together
for her birth. And a thousand ants gave their lives so that
she would have their colour and their veneer. She looks
like a carnation with many frills and is a handspan tall.
She opens for seventy night-nights: the darkest, the still-
est, the deadest of nights. They grope blindly for her, to

prepare the ointment that makes one suffer. This ointment is applied behind the ears, between the toes, on the inside of the left thigh ... Rub hard and sleep soundly, because the sickness develops on its own. At the end of two days and two nights you awaken feeling such great sorrow it won't let you breathe. A beautiful sorrow to make you feel important; a sorrow of stone and salt, a profound, bitter sorrow of liver and entrails, a sorrow that fastens on the throat like a hammered-in nail, a ten thousand kilometre sorrow; a sorrow that kills your poor heart and halts the blood there for it to rot. A sorrow that, like all the greatest sorrows, cannot be explained. Don't let it escape; if it were to get away, you would be nobody once again.

Crazy Flower

She is very sticky and very dangerous. She is on the loose, and Heaven help us. She is neither pretty nor ugly: she is a flower. She is shaped like a spider and is waxy in colour. Men's sweet blood attracts her. She waits at the roadside for them to pass by; but they have to wear long trousers. With one leap she is on their shoe, then very cautiously she crawls between trouser leg and skin, carries on upwards, and stops when she reaches the line of the knee. She clings to it and falls asleep.

Lone Flower

In a destroyed city – land of blood and oblivion and soldiers' cries – a delicate, sharp stem is born that produces flowers as round as plates. The stem has no leaves, the flower no petals, the stem pushes upwards, produces the first plate, then pierces it in the middle and carries on growing. At two metres high, another plate. It curls up as though in the palm of a hand. Two metres, and again a plate. The stem grows. Two metres, a plate, two metres a plate . . . two metres a plate, two metres a plate, two metres a plate, two metres a plate two metres a plate twometresaplatetwometresaplatetwometresaplate . . . no one knows when it ends.

Transplanted Flower

In a village of pastures, the light was filled with flowers. Flowers of the rose family, with oval, pointed leaves, spiky and rough underneath. Their colour kept changing. The whole village was in love with them and took care of them; they looked after them so much that the menfolk would forget to take the animals to the pastures, and the women would forget to light the fire and put things to cook in the pans. When night fled they all came out of their houses to water them, look at them – to pray for the flowers. Until one day the king said he had been patient enough and that these excesses had to stop. He had a thousand mule carts prepared and had the flowers transported far away from the village. Without the flowers, everybody worked. Then the plague arrived. The wise men were studying, the king was being ruined. The oxen and calves were dying. A vinegar-coloured mosquito stung the animals with a deadly bite. Until it was discovered that the perfume from the flowers they had removed from their houses kept the mosquito away, because it could not bear the scent. The king went in person to bring the flowers back, and the flowers returned to their land. In front of each bush, a sentinel. Every night, a visit from the bishop and the king. The flowers found the earth too poor and the ceremonies unpleasant. Their land wasn't their land, and they soon withered and died. Then the king had all the girls line up and sniffed them one by one. Those who smelled like flowers were taken aside and he had them planted up to their necks to see if their hair grew with the flowers. But no. And the king cried out, tearing the embroidery from his chest: 'The mosquitoes will be back!' And the bishop said: 'The mosquitoes will be back!' And they were on their way.

Phantom Flower

Neither silk nor lace, neither the threads of the lunatic moon nor the mirror of the sun on the water, nor the most delicate petal of peach tree blossom can compare to the daintiness of this flower, which can only be seen when, at midnight, on the last night of the year, the clock strikes twelve. She appears in the midst of a meadow when the grass lies frozen. She is a flower of dust and mist, the colour of honey and fingernail. She greets every chime: saluting the four points of the compass, the earth, the dying year and the year waiting on the threshold, the flower she once was before dying forever, all the other flowers that don't know her, the sleeping ant, the bird that can't be seen, the air that carried it off, and one last time to nobody: that makes a baker's dozen. Then she buries herself once more. She keeps herself warm with rotting leaves and gravel, and before burying herself for a whole year, calls out: Tralala! Her way of saying goodbye.

Sweet-Toothed Flower
Eats you alive. She catches you, folds you up, gets inside you and spits out the buttons. She absorbs you very slowly because she has poor digestion. Better that way.

Fire Flower
From a bed of pine needles she emerges in the shape of an umbrella, that is, like a mushroom. She strolls about as much as she can, which isn't much, because walking tires her. When the partridge sees her, it flies away in terror. She is a very sensible flower, who lives her life without bothering anyone. And all of a sudden on a certain day and at a certain hour, a certain moment, either because the

sun is burning or because the year has reached the highest point of light, flames appear all around her: lively flames of happiness, and this happiness makes everything catch fire. She runs around madly, whistling and spinning like a top: flying, rising, descending. Smoke comes from the bed of pine needles, from the smoke the flame is born, the flower runs and jumps, setting fire to the entire wood, and dies in the fire without comprehending how so much happiness could end in a field of ashes and charcoal.

Shadow Flower

The shadow of a flower falls to the ground. The Shadow Flower, tied to she knows not what, only lives when those who give light live. Thinner than a cigarette paper, flat, sometimes facing upwards, sometimes on her side, obliged to eat dust, without roots, blood, or bees, far from her flower, just next to her flower, all of her elephant-coloured, she stares at the constellations when they come out, because that's the only thing she can do: the glass squirrel, the mitzurica's teeth, the yolk leaf, the blue seamstress, the drummer's mouth, the sulphur boat, the soldier without hands, the hangman with the iron tongue, the salt cherry, the rooster of joy . . . When she is not even a shadow, lost in her flower, she remembers the drops of water from the sky as if they were a mirage. When the sun brings her to life, she thinks back to this. And when the moon brings her to life, she looks and looks at the black embroidery of water without even daring to breathe. But when the day is grey and the night very dark, she is neither flower nor shadow, not even the shadow of a flower. Farewell.

Shyness Flower

As the petals emerge from the bud to bloom, she shakes them off. She does not want to be a flower. She does not want to be drawn.

Pride Flower

Always the tallest in a meadow. Growing in the grass of the ditches makes her think she is someone. All the apple tree blossoms, she thinks, are her sisters, flowers of light, and that she is the only flower of the earth, daughter of the water and the sun. If the smallest boy from the farmhouse plucks her and starts to pull off her petals, she resists. Her martyrdom is like the ancient dismembering: four horses firmly tied to each limb, pulling hour after hour. Until each horse dragged away a bloody limb. If Pride Flower dies this way, she doesn't even protest.

Sadness Flower

Her leaves the colour of rat skin, she opens on rainy afternoons when the acacias are a honey-smelling sea. Opened to the dimmest light, she sighs and weeps. If she had hands you would say 'Here' and lend her a handkerchief. If you tiptoe away, tired of this play-acting, you will hear her tiny sobs. If you stride off, she becomes frightened and falls silent. If you say 'Poor thing' to her, you're done for. It's best not to pay her much attention, and to look at her unenthusiastically, wait for her to get tired and to carry on with her growing, because she hasn't the heart to do anything else.

Locust Flower

The Locust Flower jumps on you. She is shaped like an orchid, and coloured as if made of custard. If you stray absent-mindedly into a garden or wood, it's a surprise. The first time – if you are unaware – it's a distressing surprise. Pow! And she is already stuck to you. She doesn't consider anything. Sticks wherever she likes. Like a butterfly with its wings pinned in a glass case, she doesn't move until she withers and dies. Three of them can jump on you, not more. Pow! One. Pow! Two. Pow! Three. Don't even think about it. Even if you whistle softly to them and call them by affectionate names, it's no use. Three is the most they must think you can have on you. What's saddest of all is that this measured concern is without perfume.

Drop-Of-Bile Flower

Hides under leaves. Many years passed before her shape became known. And her colour. The colour of moon and star. Because those who speak of her speak of a memory. A flower with a single petal: a plant tongue. You're walking along and suddenly think: where does all this smell come from? This flower's perfume cannot be compared to any other, and perhaps because it is the colour of the moon, the full moon brings it out. Then you may as well die. Intense. You want to pick the hidden flower . . . The perfume leads you on. You approach, sense that the flower is close by, but you can never find her. With your hand you push aside leaves and more heavy, velvety leaves, searching and searching . . . When she wants, she appears from behind the most unexpected leaf, and attacks. Plop! A fine drop of bile. Then she hides again. Many people say she doesn't hide, but that, bled dry, she dies. The drop of bile is harmless. It won't stain clothes or skin. But if it gets in your eye, you're done for. It's like whiplash. And for the rest of your life you won't see more than a few inches in front of your nose.

Delirium Flower

The plant of this flower is a tender climber. It produces bunches of flowers quite similar to wisteria, but they flower first at the tip – the opposite of wisteria, which begin to flower at the bottom. The flower is white, with a bluish tinge, as if she had been put to wash with blue items. She is thimble-shaped. The three-pointed pistil is the foot of the plant. As soon as the first flower opens, the bunch extends, all the flowers start opening, and the bunch doesn't stop extending until the first flower touches the ground with one foot. Then the bunch bends, the flowers droop down to the ground and stay like that, feet in the soil. The thimble dries out and a new shoot sprouts from each foot. If you're not careful, she invades your house both inside and out, and that of your neighbours as well. It's terrible.

Fancy Dress Flower

Like those insects that, through fear, assume the colour of the branch they are on, this flower takes on the colour of the wall where she is born. A bird drops the seed – she needs the help of a bird (the wild merlin) – on a ledge, or in a crack. She grows and lives there, at the tip of a slender stem, curled and flexible, a bell-shaped flower, pure spirit. When it is dark night, she climbs to your balcony or your window and puts you to sleep if you are awake, so that she can direct your dreams while you sleep. She whispers in your ear that there's no one in the world like you and that everything around you is deceit. Only you are pure and high-minded. There is nothing clean. Everything is worm-eaten: brother, wife, friends. Each night she does the same. Until you detest everything, until you can't live without her, until you yearn for her, until you become alone with your soul and the flower. Once you are completely hers, she gives a shake, uproots herself, and disappears. The only way to save yourself is to spot her in time and to water her with sugar soap.

Wounded Flower

The Wounded Flower is a robust flower. A long time ago, she grew in valleys, in the shade of grass and trees. Then the wind, crazy as ever, began to carry her seeds up high and scatter them on the slopes of volcanoes. That wouldn't matter were it not for the bird Perdingues. The flower has five lemon-coloured petals that are long and stiff, and the pistil is a kind of grassy sword, pale green in colour. The flower is small, and the plant looks like any other grass. The bird, which has more senses than necessary, knows when the flower should open, and starts flying over her in tight circles, as soon as the bud starts forming. As soon as she opens, it swoops on her and, from up above, tears off two petals. The one closest to its beak and the one furthest away. Just two. As each petal is pulled off it has been discovered that the flower says: Ow! The bird flies off squawking and half an hour later bursts. The flower's three remaining petals are never touched by any other bird: a dreadful smell comes from the wounds. And the joke is repeated the next year.

Jealous Flower

The explorer who sought to acclimatise her had no idea what she was like. He planted the only seed he had under his bedroom window. The next morning he saw a tiny shoot emerging from the ground shaking like jelly. The day after that he saw another one alongside the first. A shoot was born every day, first on one side, then on the other of the motherfather seed, in a very regimented manner. The first shoots were already tall by the time the last ones were born. Pure delight. And the man was contented. The entire lower part of the house was a green cloud of leaves that at the slightest breeze began to tremble delicately: more graceful and transparent than a fly's wing. The day the flowers opened the sun delayed a little its setting: it was in awe of her. The scent produced had an enchanting freshness. All round the house was a joyous celebration. But beneath all this joy, a hell was at work. The roots of the flower-bearing plants seemed to be centuries old, and began to disturb the house from underneath – it was in their way. They coveted the ground the house occupied. They wanted everything: the absolute. The right-hand side of the house subsided. A portion of the roof balustrade collapsed. One of the shutters fell off. One night it was as if they were shaking the house to death. When daylight came, the house was far away. It had fled in terror.

Strolling Flower

From twin bulbs joined at the top, is born a three-pointed silver flower, striped blue, noble as can be. The bulbs are her feet. These feet have short roots that don't dig deep into the ground: they are only supports. The Strolling Flower is whimsical, vagabond. She never travels alone. She cannot live without company. They move about in groups. Enjoy the sunshine. They flee shade like the plague and walk like ducks. If they like the place where they have chosen to grow, all well and good. However, if due to a lack of rain the ground has dried out too much, since their life depends on it, slowly, slowly, they all head for the ditch. They soon become friends with the stinking clover. They last a summer, whether they are in a valley or on a hill, beneath a fence or in the middle of a meadow. As soon as autumn arrives, they get together six by six and whisper secrets to each other. When they separate for the winter goodbye, they still look good even though their colours have paled a little. They hide to die: they look for old trees and shelter in their trunks, they slip under moss that never completely covers them, or under bark. Wherever they can. At the first icy blast they are finished. With a very skilful, careful shake, their feet bring down the stem and the flower. They cast off a corpse as indifferently as we cast off an old piece of clothing.

Sick Flower

Hides her little mouth – covers it with the smallest leaves. Every so often the leaves separate, blue smoke comes out of her mouth, and she whistles. Very softly. To keep her company the starflowers send her fragrance, and the rain showers her so that she won't be sad. This is how she lives and dies: surrounded by affection and kindness.

Sponge Finger Flower

She is made with her little head twisted and pointing down. If she had been given eyes she could count the little creatures on the flat ground. Is almost worthless. If you make a bouquet of them, five minutes later the leaves fall off. But she is very pretty and, if you crouch down, you can see her insides: they are the colour of violin rosin, and so are the stamens.

Arrow Flower

No one knows where they come from. Then suddenly they go, and it's as if they've gone for ever. But one fine day they're back, they take over large plots of land and occasionally a lonely garden. The plant looks like a sun-flower: tall, with rough, broad leaves. Arrow flowers can be yellow, red, blue, carrot-coloured, or purple as if gasping for breath. They look as if they're made of satin. They point to the sky. If it's windy, the whole plant bends over.

The flower does the same, and the wind doesn't harm her. If it's raining, they cut through the rain: the drops run quickly down their sides and varnish them. And when they have lived long enough, the plant shoots out the flower violently. A mixture of colours and happiness flies skywards. They don't do any harm. They fly high and disappear. Until next year.

Honey Flower

Her calyx is filled with honey. She is a sleeping flower, somehow outside of time. The bees come and go. They draw closer. With their spoon legs they collect honey and fill pots and pans. Some of them die drowned in honey. Everything happens in a rush, in a great commotion. When the calyx is emptied of honey and the flower can breathe, she dies. Then new ones are born. Bring on the bees!

Fossil Flower

Scared to death, a strawberry flower was lost and didn't know what to do. Veins of gold were burning. Black sulphur and red dust, white earth and shiny charcoal were splitting apart. And on the slopes where, inside, world and sea were still boiling, jets of water rose to the sky. Coloured stones were born, to the cries of lizards with frills from head to tail. The strawberry flower couldn't do anything facing or turning its back on the lime, clay, or stone ... When everything calmed down, the trees looked like crosses. Pierced by ice and fire, a piece of blue breathed unhealthily on the summit of a cleft mountain. Lost and wounded, the strawberry flower was left without air: surrounded by dust and liquid, little by little she choked. The water and mud were turning to stone. The suffocating strawberry flower began to change . . . a thousand years . . . a million years . . . changing . . . three million years . . . until she was nothing: a slow imprisoned defeat . . . an emptiness in a stone . . . an indent.

TRANSLATORS' NOTE

Mercè Rodoreda is widely recognised as the pre-eminent writer in Catalan of the twentieth century. Born in 1908 and brought up in Barcelona, during the first half of the 1930s she was an enthusiastic supporter of Catalan culture, and the author of several novels and articles for newspapers and magazines. As so many others experienced, Rodoreda had her life split in two by the Civil War of 1936 to 1939. Advised for her own safety to leave Catalonia towards the end of the conflict, she lived in exile in France and Switzerland for over thirty years.

She described her feelings as she looked back on those years in an interview for the magazine *Serra d'Or*:

> The pre-war world seemed unreal to me, and I still haven't reconstructed it. And the time I spent! Everything

burned inside. But imperceptibly it was becoming a little anachronistic. And perhaps this is what hurt most. I couldn't have written a novel if they'd beaten it out of me. I was too disconnected from everything, or maybe too bound up with everything, though that might sound like a paradox.

Despite this, in the late 1950s Rodoreda began to write again, producing first a volume of short stories, then following it with *La mort i la primavera* (*Death in Spring*, 1986, the novel that she started writing in 1961 and was published, posthumously and unfinished, in 1986) described by Sarah Moss as 'dark, beautiful and brilliant', and in 1962 came *La plaça del Diamant* (often described as the best Catalan novel ever written and variously published in English as *The Time of the Doves* and *The Pigeon Girl*, and most recently as *In Diamond Square*). The last work published before her death was *Quanta, quanta guerra* (published in 1980 and then in English in 2015 as *War, So Much War*), written in Catalonia having returned from exile in 1972.

As she grew older, Rodoreda turned away from the psychological realism of her earlier novels and began to write texts where magic, symbolism and dreams come to the fore. Nowhere is this more evident than in *Journeys and Flowers* (*Viatges i flors*), first published in Catalan in 1980, and one of the few books of hers not previously published in English. Describing why she wrote these short surreal pieces, Mercè Rodoreda told her editor and friend Joan Sales: 'I'm tired to the depths of my soul of revolutions, coups, civil wars, great wars, concentration camps, napalm bombings, torture, kidnappings, social struggles, the madness for giving orders that men have, especially those who don't have any ability to give them.'

The language Rodoreda uses to convey these journeys and flowers is unique. Her allegorical, oneiric style is reminiscent of folk tales and fables: the ever-changing metaphorical levels present a distorting mirror that shows hidden aspects of life in a way that mingles the grotesque with the comic. It is a luminous and dark universe in equal parts. Tender and cruel in the same measure. From a popular, not at all self-conscious language, to one that is expert in botany, gardening, literature, history. Her 'Journeys' take the reader through the agonising experience of exile, filled with destruction and desolation; her anthropomorphic 'Flowers', which are almost always female, offer the reader both a possible and an impossible world.

Journeys and Flowers invites the reader into a dream world where the unconscious offers insights into our ways of interpreting existence. We might think of the poems of the French Surrealists and the writer Henri Michaux, as well as work by contemporary authors like Max Porter, Irene Solà or Blanca Llum Vidal, and also performance artists such as Cabosanroque. We are under Rodoreda's influence, hypnotised. Dreaming, perhaps? But daydreaming, as if with a fever.

Translating Rodoreda does not simply mean to translate words from Catalan to English. It is to be ever alert to her own special language. Rodoreda chooses words as richly and confidently as an experienced hiker takes different plant cuttings here and there, and other small mementos of her travels, a small branch, a dried fruit, or a fossilised shell. Our process of translation also involves discarding other words, like the walker who kicks the small stones on the path, confident they are of no use.

It could be said that Mercè Rodoreda's Catalan is not too far from the virtues of English language, as it is concise and devoid of affectation. But to precisely convey that particularity, that economy of language, that unique specificity that is Rodoreda's Catalan into English constantly raises questions of finding the right tone. It is not only a matter of choosing the right words, but of conveying the author's unique voice. For hints on how to answer these and other questions we looked, among many other things, at Edward Burne-Jones's *The Flower Book* and Edward Lear's *Nonsense Botany*.

The texture of Rodoreda's prose must pulsate through the pages in this book, even when it appears awkward or impenetrable. The aromas of the Mediterranean, the character of its people, the history and sorrows of its Catalan villages, everything must resonate on the page and transport the reader to the past and to the future. The reader becomes Rodoreda's inquisitive narrator, a pilgrim in strange lands, an insect, or a flower. Even though none of this has ever existed, it becomes real in our imagination.

These texts are a rich example of Rodoreda's writing at its most genuine: one that reveals the radical impulses of life with humour and bold imagination, but employing a language that engages the reader with its apparent simplicity, combining inventive force and lyrical power in a poetic voice of indelible magnetism. She herself said: 'If they asked me which of my books I wanted to save from a fire, I would choose this one.' Our task as translators has been, as the pilgrim of her 'Journeys' says: 'not to stop but to carry on for ever; to continue the endless hunt for dark hearts and unknown traditions.'

Gala Sicart Olavide and Nick Caistor
London, April 2024

Daunt Books

Founded in 2010, Daunt Books Publishing grew out of Daunt Books, independent booksellers with shops in London and the south of England. We publish the finest writing in English and in translation, from literary fiction – novels and short stories – to narrative non-fiction, including essays and memoirs. Our modern classics list revives authors whose work has unjustly fallen out of print. In 2020 we launched Daunt Books Originals, an imprint for bold and inventive new writing.

www.dauntbookspublishing.co.uk